ASTERIX AND THE LAUREL WREATH

TEXT BY GOSCINNY

DRAWINGS BY UDERZO

TRANSLATED BY ANTHEA BELL AND DEREK HOCKRIDGE

HODDER DARGAUD
LONDON SYDNEY AUCKLAND

ASTERIX IN OTHER COUNTRIES

Australia	Hodder Dargaud, Rydalmere Business Park, 10/16 South Street, Rydalmere, N.S.W. 2116, Australia
Austria	Delta Verlag GmbH, Postfach 10 12 45, 70011 Stuttgart, Germany
Belarus	Egmont Belarus, Mogilevskaya 43, 220007 Minsk, Belarus
Belgium	Dargaud Benelux, 17 Avenue Paul Henri Spaak, 1070 Brussels, Belgium
Brazil	Record Distribuidora, Rua Argentina 171, 20921 Rio de Janeiro, Brazil
Bulgaria	Egmont Bulgaria Ltd., U1. Sweta Gora 7, IV et.,1421 Sofia, Bulgaria
Canada	(*French*) Presse-Import Leo Brunelle Inc., 5757 rue Cypihot, St. Laurent, QC, H4S 1X4, Canada
	(*English*) General Publishing Co. Ltd., 30 Lesmill Road, Don Mills, Ontario M38 2T6, Canada
Corsica	Dargaud Editeur, 6 rue Gager Gabillot, 75015 Paris, France
Croatia	Izvori Publishing House, Trnjanska 47, 4100 Zagreb, Croatia
Czech Republic	Egmont CR, Hellichova 45, 118 00 Prague 1, Czech Republic
Denmark	Serieforlaget A/S (Egmont Group), Vognmagergade 11, 1148 Copenhagen K, Denmark
Estonia	Egmont Estonia Ltd., Hobujaamal, EE 0001 Tallinn, Estonia
Finland	Sanoma Corporation/Helsinki Media, POB 107, 00381 Helsinki, Finland
France	Dargaud Editeur, 6 rue Gager Gabillot, 75015 Paris, France
	(*titles up to and including Asterix in Belgium*)
	Les Editions Albert Rene, 26 Avenue Victor Hugo, 75116 Paris, France
	(*titles from Asterix and the Great Divide onwards*)
Germany	Delta Verlag GmbH, Postfach 10 12 45, 70011 Stuttgart, Germany
Greece	(*Ancient and Modern Greek*) Mamouth Comix Ltd., 44 Ippokratous St., 106080 Athens, Greece
Holland	Dargaud Benelux, 17 Avenue Paul Henri Spaak, 1070 Brussels, Belgium
	(*Distribution*) Betapress, Burg. Krollaan 14, 5126 PT Jilze, Holland
Hong Kong	(*English*) Hodder Dargaud, c/o Publishers Associates Ltd., 11th Floor, Taikoo Trading Estate, 28 Tong Cheong Street, Quarry Bay, Hong Kong
	(*Mandarin and Cantonese*) Gast, Fairyland Garden 6A, Broadcast Drive 8, Kowloon Tong, Hong Kong
Hungary	Egmont Hungary Kft., Karolina ut. 65, 1113 Budapest, Hungary
India	(*Bengali*) Ananda Publishers, 45 Beniatola Lane, Calcutta 700 009, India
Indonesia	PT. Pustaka Sinar Harapan, Jl. Dewi Sartika 136D, Cawang, Jakarta 13630, Indonesia
Israel	Dahlia Pelled Publishers Ltd., Pinsker 64, Tel Aviv 61116, Israel
Italy	Mondadori, Via A. Mondadori 15, 37131 Verona, Italy
Republic of Korea	Cosmos Editions, 19–16 Shin An-dong, Jin-ju, Gyung Nam-do, Republic of Korea
Latin America	Grijalbo-Dargaud, Aragon 385, 08013 Barcelona, Spain
Latvia	Egmont Latvia Ltd., Balasta Dambis 3, Room 1812, 226081 Riga, Latvia
Lithuania	Egmont Lithuania, Juozapaviciaus 9 A, Room 910/911, 2600 Vilnius, Lithuania
Luxembourg	Imprimerie St. Paul, rue Christophe Plantin 2, Luxembourg
New Zealand	Hodder Dargaud, P.O. Box 3858, Auckland 1, New Zealand
Norway	A/S Hjemmet – Serieforlaget, PB 6853 St. Olavs Pl. 0130 Oslo, Norway
Poland	Egmont Polska Ltd., Plac Marszalka J. Pilsudskiego 9, 00–078 Warsaw, Poland
Portugal	Meriberica-Liber, Av. Alvares Cabral 84, R/C-D 1200 Lisbon, Portugal
Roman Empire	(*Latin*) Delta Verlag GmbH, Postfach 10 12 45, 70011 Stuttgart, Germany
Romania	Egmont Romania S.R.L., Calea Grivitei 160, Ap. 47; Cod 78214, Sector 1, Bucharest, Romania
Russia	Egmont Russia, 9, 1st Smolenski per. 121099 Moscow, Russia
Slovak Republic	Egmont Neografia Nevädzova 8, Box 20, 82799 Bratislava 27, Slovak Republic
Slovenia	Didakta, Radovljica Kranjska Cesta 13, 64240 Radovljica, Slovenia
South Africa	(*English*) Hodder Dargaud, c/o Struik Book Distributors (Pty) Ltd., Graph Avenue, Montague Gardens 7441, South Africa
	(*Afrikaans*) Human & Rousseau (Pty) Ltd., State House, 3–9 Rose Street, Cape Town 8000, South Africa
Spain	(*Castillian, Catalan, Basque*) Grijalbo-Dargaud, Aragon 385, 08013 Barcelona, Spain
Sweden	Serieförlaget Svenska AB (Egmont Group), 212 05 Malmö, Sweden
Switzerland	Dargaud (Suisse) S.A., En Budron B-13, 1052 Le Mont sur Lausanne, Switzerland
Turkey	Remzi Kitabevi, Selvili Mescit S. 3, Cagaloglu-Istanbul, Turkey
USA	(*English and French language distributor*) Presse-Import Leo Brunelle Inc., 5757 rue Cypihot, St. Laurent, QC, H4S 1X4, Canada

Asterix and the Laurel Wreath

ISBN 0 340 19107 4 (cased)
ISBN 0 340 20699 3 (limp)

First published in Great Britain 1974 (cased)
This impression 95 96 97 98

First published in Great Britain 1976 (limp)
This impression 95 96 97 98

Published by Hodder Dargaud Ltd,
338 Euston Road, London NW1 3BH

Printed in Belgium by Proost International Book Production

GAULISH VILLAGE

COMPENDIUM

LAUDANUM

AQUARIUM

TOTORUM

ARMORICA

BELGICA

LUTETIA

SPQR

GAUL
(ROMAN CONQUEST)
50 B.C.

CELTICA

PROVINCIA

AQUITANIA

The year is 50 BC. Gaul is entirely occupied by the Romans. Well, not entirely... One small village of indomitable Gauls still holds out against the invaders. And life is not easy for the Roman legionaries who garrison the fortified camps of Totorum, Aquarium, Laudanum and Compendium...

a few of the Gauls

Asterix, the hero of these adventures. A shrewd, cunning little warrior; all perilous missions are immediately entrusted to him. Asterix gets his superhuman strength from the magic potion brewed by the druid Getafix…

Obelix, Asterix's inseparable friend. A menhir delivery-man by trade; addicted to wild boar. Obelix is always ready to drop everything and go off on a new adventure with Asterix — so long as there's wild boar to eat, and plenty of fighting.

Getafix, the venerable village druid. Gathers mistletoe and brews magic potions. His speciality is the potion which gives the drinker superhuman strength. But Getafix also has other recipes up his sleeve…

Cacofonix, the bard. Opinion is divided as to his musical gifts. Cacofonix thinks he's a genius. Everyone else thinks he's unspeakable. But so long as he doesn't speak, let alone sing, everybody likes him…

Finally, Vitalstatistix, the chief of the tribe. Majestic, brave and hot-tempered, the old warrior is respected by his men and feared by his enemies. Vitalstatistix himself has only one fear; he is afraid the sky may fall on his head tomorrow. But as he always says, 'Tomorrow never comes.'

ANOTHER SUNNY DAY HAS JUST DAWNED UPON THE GREATEST CITY IN THE UNIVERSE **ROME.**

ALTHOUGH, BY CÆSAR'S DECREE, TRAFFIC IS NOT ALLOWED ON THE STREETS IN THE DAYTIME, THE CITY IS INCREDIBLY NOISY, CROWDED WITH SHOPKEEPERS AND STREETSELLERS CRYING THEIR WARES... FRUCTUARII, PEPONARII, OLITORES, PISCATORES, VINARII, SILIGINARII, PASTILLARII...

CAKES!

TRY MY VEGETABLES! NICE WHOLESOME VEG!

FISH! GOOD FRESH FISH!

EAT MORE FRUIT!

RIPE JUICY MELONS!

SWEETS!

THE PASSERS-BY ARE BESET BY BEGGARS AND FLAG SELLERS...

HAVE PITY ON A POOR GLADIATOR IN REDUCED CIRCUMSTANCES!

DON'T YOU WANT TO SUPPORT A GOOD CAUSE THEN?

TOURISTS FROM ALL OVER THE WORLD, THRACIANS, GOTHS, BRITONS, EGYPTIANS, SICAMBRES, ETHIOPIANS, NUMIDIANS, ALL ADD TO THE LOCAL COLOUR...

AND HERE WE HAVE THE CIRCUS MAXIMUS... AND HERE WE HAVE THE CIRCUS MAXIMUS...

and here we have the Circus Maximus

IN FACT, EVERYTHING LEADS US TO BELIEVE THAT WE MAY SEE EVEN STRANGER SIGHTS AROUND THE NEXT CORNER...

5

IN SPITE OF THE FACT THAT TRAFFIC IS FORBIDDEN, THE STREETS OF LUTETIA ARE NOISY. NOISY BUT CHEERFUL, THANKS TO THE INSPIRED REPARTEE SO TYPICAL OF THE LUTETIAN SENSE OF HUMOUR...

I'VE GOT A JOB TO DO. I HAVE!

IDIOT!

FOOL!

MORON!

YOUNG HOOLIGAN!

HALF-WIT!

GO ON, YOU CAN GET THROUGH!

NO, I CAN'T!

I'M TELLING YOU YOU CAN!

DO YOU REALLY THINK SO?

THERE, WHAT DID I TELL YOU?

LET US TAKE A CLOSER LOOK AT THIS LITTLE GROUP OF VISITORS UP FROM THE COUNTRY...

LOOK HERE, IMPEDIMENTA, COMING TO LUTETIA TO DO YOUR SHOPPING IS ONE THING, BUT GOING TO SEE HOMEOPATHIX IS ANOTHER! DO WE REALLY HAVE TO?

WELL, I CAN HARDLY VISIT LUTETIA WITHOUT CALLING ON MY BROTHER, CAN I? ANYWAY, HE'S INVITED US TO DINNER.

YOU KNOW VERY WELL HOMEOPATHIX AND I DON'T GET ON!

OH, OF COURSE, WHEN IT'S A MEMBER OF MY FAMILY...

3A

HOMEOPATHIX HAS GOT TO THE TOP, HE HAS! HIS WIFE DOESN'T LIVE IN A VILLAGE OF MADMEN, SURROUNDED BY ROMANS.

AND DID YOU HAVE TO ASK THOSE TWO TO COME ALONG?

?

I MAY NOT HAVE GOT TO THE TOP, BUT I AM A CHIEF! AND A CHIEF NEEDS HIS ESCORT... ASTERIX AND OBELIX ARE MY BEST MEN! MY GUARD OF HONOUR!

WELL, I HOPE YOUR GUARD OF HONOUR KNOWS HOW TO BEHAVE ITSELF, THAT'S ALL. HERE WE ARE!

RHUBARB RHUBARB B GUARD OF HONOUR RHUBARB RHUBARB RHUBARB RHUBARB RHUBARB AND DO YOU KNOW WHAT MY GUARD OF HONOUR SAYS TO YOU...

KNOCK!
KNOCK!
KNOCK!

3B

LITTLE PEDIMENTA!

HOMEOPATHIKINS!

TAPIOCA! TAPIOCA! IMPEDIMENTA AND WHATSISNAME HAVE ARRIVED!

WHATSISNAME? **WHAT DO YOU MEAN, WHATSISNAME?**

I'VE BROUGHT YOU ONE OF OUR SEASIDE SHELLS... VITALSTATISTIX WANTED TO BRING YOU A MENHIR, THE SAME AS USUAL.

BUT MY DEAR CHAP, WHERE AM I GOING TO PUT THESE MENHIRS OF YOURS?

YOU REALLY WANT ME TO TELL YOU?

VITALSTA-TISTIX!

OH, HOW LOVELY IT IS HERE!

YES, I'VE REDECORATED THE WHOLE PLACE. I WAS GETTING TIRED OF COUNTRY STUFF... TAPIOCA, LET'S HAVE A DRINK.

TRY SOME OF THE 55 B.C., FROM OUR OWN VINEYARD. IT'S A MODEST, UNPRETENTIOUS LITTLE WINE, BUT I HOPE YOU LIKE IT.

HOW'S BUSINESS, HOMEOPATHIX? STILL GOOD?

EXCELLENT! I'M ABOUT TO OPEN BRANCHES AT LUGDUNUM AND MASSILIA...

HOW FASCINATING! AND WILL YOU BE DOING MUCH TRAVELLING?

NOT IF I CAN HELP IT! WHEN A MAN IS TIRED OF LUTETIA, HE IS TIRED OF LIFE. THE REST OF GAUL IS ONLY FIT FOR BOARS

LET'S HAVE SOME MORE OF THE 55 B.C., OBELIX. AT LEAST THAT'S MODEST AND UNPRETENTIOUS.

?

CENA IS SERVED!

OH, TAPIOCA, HOW WONDERFUL!

OF COURSE, IT MUST BE A BIT OF A CHANGE FROM THE STUFF YOU GET TO EAT AT HOME!

AND WHAT'S WRONG WITH WHAT WE GET TO EAT AT HOME?

NOTHING, EXCEPT I DON'T OFTEN HAVE BEAVERS' TAILS IN STRAWBERRY SAUCE AT HOME!

HEY, OBELIX! PASS THE WINE, WILL YOU?

NOW, WHATSYOURNAME, HOW ABOUT SOME COW'S HOOF MOULD? I BET YOU'VE NEVER HAD ANYTHING LIKE THIS...

YOU DON'T IMPRESS ME WITH YOUR COW'S HOOF MOULD! YOU'RE JUST MAKING PIGS OF YOURSELVES!

VITALSTATISTIX, DON'T BE SUCH A BOOR!

WELL, AT LEAST I CAN BRING HOME THE BACON!

HOMEOPATHIX!

DID MADAM CALL?

YES. MORE WINE, PLEASE.

WELL, I MAY NOT HAVE YOUR MONEY, BUT I DO HAVE HONOUR AND GLORY INSTEAD!

AND DOES HONOUR AND GLORY PROVIDE YOU WITH COW'S HOOF MOULD, DEAR BROTHER-IN-LAW?

SEE THAT? THAT'S JULIUS CAESAR'S PALACE.

SO WE JUST MASSACRE THE GUARD, AND ONCE INSIDE THE PALACE WE ASK OUR WAY TO CAESAR'S LAUREL WREATH, WHICH WE NEED TO SEASON A STEW...

...AND HAVING GOT OUR HANDS ON THE LAUREL WREATH WE SIMPLY BASH OUR WAY OUT AND GO HOME. RIGHT?

RIGHT! COMING?

OBELIX, THOSE LEGIONARIES IN CAESAR'S PALACE ARE A TOUGHER PROPOSITION THAN THE SORT WE GET AT HOME...AND THE MAGIC POTION DOESN'T MAKE US INVULNERABLE. WE MUST THINK OF SOMETHING ELSE.

THAT MAN JUST CAME OUT OF THE PALACE. HE MIGHT BE ABLE TO TELL US HOW TO GET IN. LET'S FOLLOW HIM.

BUT... HE MAY KNOW THE WAY OUT, BUT THAT DOESN'T MEAN TO SAY HE KNOWS THE WAY IN, AND...

EXCUSE ME! WE'RE STRANGERS HERE, AND WE'D LIKE TO ASK YOU A FEW QUESTIONS.

I'M A BUSY MAN GAUL...

HOW ABOUT GOING IN HERE FOR A LITTLE DRINK?

I DON'T REALLY KNOW IF I CAN...

JUST AS I THOUGHT! HE CAN GET OUT OF PLACES ALL RIGHT, BUT HE'S NOT SO GOOD AT GETTING IN.

TABERNA BIBULUS

WE DON'T WANT TO BUY, WE WANT TO SELL.

SELL! OH, THAT'S DIFFERENT...

IF YOU'RE IN THE TRADE I CAN ONLY SEE YOU FIRST THING IN THE MORNING... WELL, AND WHO DID YOU HAVE TO OFFER ME?

US.

YOU? I DON'T GO BUYING ANY OLD THING.

WE'RE NOT ANY OLD THING!

THIS ONE SMELLS OF WINE.

WELL, YES, BUT HE ONLY INDULGES ONCE IN A WHILE... AND HE'S VERY STRONG.

SHOW US HOW STRONG YOU ARE OBELIX!

RIGHT.

PAF!

YES, YES... BUT I SPECIALIZE IN ELEGANT STUFF I'M EXPECTING THE PALACE MAJOR-DOMO ANY MINUTE, LET ME TELL YOU. HE'S COMING TO BUY SOME SLAVES...

SCHLONK!

I'M VERY STRONG TOO. WANT ME TO SHOW YOU?

NO! NO! DON'T BOTHER... MAFTER, I'M FURE THEY WON'T FPOIL THE DIFPLAY...

RIGHT, I'LL TAKE YOU, BUT ONLY ON SALE OR RETURN. IF I DON'T SELL YOU TODAY, YOU CAN GO AND GET SOLD SOMEWHERE ELSE.

FOLLOW ME.

THE HOUSE OF TYPHVS

ONCE INSIDE CAESAR'S PALACE, WE'LL SET ABOUT LOOKING FOR HIS LAURELS!

SO LONG AS HE ISN'T RESTING ON THEM!

SOON AFTERWARDS...

HERE WE ARE.

HEY, ASTERIX... THIS ISN'T CAESAR'S PALACE, IS IT?

PERHAPS HE HAS SEVERAL...

FIBULA! TIBIA! NITWIT! COME AND LOOK AT THIS!

SEE THESE GAULS? I GOT THEM FROM THE HOUSE OF TYPHUS.

THE HOUSE OF TYPHUS? YOU MUST BE MAD, OSSEUS! HE'S TERRIBLY EXPENSIVE.

AND WHEN I THINK OF THE FUSS THEY KICK UP IN THIS DOMUS WHEN I WANT TO BUY A NEW TOGA!

IS THAT WHAT ALL THE SHOUTING WAS ABOUT?

I THOUGHT IT WOULD BE A NICE SURPRISE.. THEY'RE RATHER AMUSING.

OH WELL, I'M GOING BACK TO MY CUBICULUM TO GET A BIT OF SLEEP.

YOU'VE BEEN OUT DRINKING ALL NIGHT WITH YOUR FRIENDS AGAIN! YOU'LL FIND YOURSELF IN MY LIBRI NIGRI✳ IF YOU DON'T WATCH OUT!

I SAY... ISN'T THIS CAESAR'S PALACE?

✳ BLACK BOOKS

CAESAR'S PALACE?

YOU'RE RIGHT, THEY ARE AMUSING!

WHY, NO, GAUL! THIS ISN'T CAESAR'S PALACE! THIS HOUSE BELONGS TO ME, OSSEUS HUMERUS...

AND THIS IS MY WIFE FIBULA, MY DAUGHTER TIBIA, AND MY NITWIT OF A SON, METATARSUS.

??

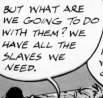

BUT WHAT ARE WE GOING TO DO WITH THEM? WE HAVE ALL THE SLAVES WE NEED.

THEY COULD WORK IN THE KITCHEN. GAULISH CUISINE IS GOOD... ANYWAY, IT CAN'T BE ANY WORSE THAN WHAT OUR BRITISH SLAVE AUTODIDAX GIVES US.

GOLDEN- DELICIUS!

YES, MASTER?

GOLDENDELICIUS, TAKE THESE TWO GAULISH SLAVES TO THE KITCHEN. THEY ARE TO PREPARE OUR MEALS.

GO WITH OUR MAJOR-DOMO, GOLDENDELICIUS.

LOOK HERE...

AND TAKE CARE OF THEM. THEY'RE FROM THE HOUSE OF TYPHUS!

WELL, THIS IS ALL YOURS, YOU TWO PRECIOUS WORKS OF ART!

TWO WHAT?

WORKS OF ART! I'M NOT A WORK OF ART FROM THE HOUSE OF TYPHUS, NOT ME! I'M NOT FRAGILE LIKE YOU, BUT THIS IS A GOOD JOB I'VE GOT HERE, EVEN IF IT IS IN A MADHOUSE...

AND DON'T YOU GO TRYING TO EDGE ME OUT OF IT!

THAT ROMAN IS CRAZY! THIS IS THE FIRST TIME ANYONE EVER TOLD ME I WAS FRAGILE!

SLAM!

TOC! TOC! TOC!

WE'VE MADE A MISTAKE... ALL THIS IS ONLY TAKING US FURTHER AWAY FROM CAESAR'S LAUREL WREATH.

WELL THEN, LET'S GO.

NO. WE'RE SLAVES. IF WE RUN AWAY WE'LL NEVER HAVE A CHANCE OF GETTING INTO CAESAR'S PALACE.

WE MUST PERSUADE HUMERUS TO RETURN US TO TYPHUS TO BE RESOLD.

JUST LIKE THE PEOPLE WHO BUY YOUR MENHIRS AND BRING THEM BACK, BECAUSE THEY'RE NOT SATISFIED.

ALL MY CUSTOMERS ARE SATISFIED!

AH, BUT YOUR MENHIRS DON'T DO THE COOKING...

WE'LL MAKE THEM A MEAL THEY WON'T FORGET IN A HURRY, BY TOUTATIS! BRING ME EVERYTHING YOU CAN FIND IN THE LARDER!

HERE YOU ARE! JAM, BLACK PEPPERCORNS, SALT, KIDNEYS, CARBOLIX SOAP, A CHICKEN, HONEY, RED PEPPERS, BLACK PUDDING, EGGS, AND POMEGRANATE SEEDS!

I'VE FOUND SOME MORE RED PEPPERS AND BLACK PEPPERCORNS... WE'LL FLING IT ALL IN THE POT!

HOW ABOUT THE CHICKEN? SHALL I PLUCK IT?

WHY BOTHER?

SOON AFTERWARDS...

IT'S NEARLY DONE.

CAN I HAVE A TASTE?

METATARSUS! GET OUT OF YOUR CUBICULUM AND COME INTO THE TRICLINIUM! CENA IS SERVED!

LOOK, I'LL DO ANYTHING, ANYTHING, ONLY DON'T SHOUT LIKE THAT... I'D FEEL BETTER FLAT ON MY CUBILE, BUT IF...

THE FACT THAT YOU HAVE MANAGED TO DECUBILATE YOURSELF GIVES YOU NO RIGHT TO BEHAVE BADLY. LIE DOWN TO THE TABLE PROPERLY.

IT DOES SMELL FUNNY...

NOT FOR ME, THANKS.

THIS MEAL WAS COOKED BY MY TWO GAULS FROM THE HOUSE OF TYPHUS! YOU'LL EAT IT AND LIKE IT!!!

GLOD!

etc...

TEEHEE HEE!

SCRUNCH! SCRUNCH!

WHERE ARE THEY? WHERE ARE THEY?

OBELIX, I RATHER THINK THE MOMENT HAS COME TO SELL OUR LIVES DEARLY!

DIDN'T WE SELL THEM BEFORE?

COME TO MY ARMS!

YOUR MIRACULOUS DISH HAS CURED ME LIKE A SHOT!

THANKS TO YOU TWO, I'LL BE ABLE TO SPEND THE NIGHT DRINKING AND MAKING MERRY WITH MY FRIENDS, HAPPY IN THE KNOWLEDGE THAT NEXT DAY YOU WILL COOK UP THIS EXCELLENT CONCOCTION TO MAKE A NEW MAN OF ME!

COME ON! COME ON! THE FAMILY WANTS TO CONGRATULATE YOU!

HEY, PATER, PATER! WE DON'T OFTEN SEE OCULUS TO OCULUS, BUT YOU REALLY WERE INSPIRED WHEN YOU BOUGHT THESE TWO THEY'RE MARVELS!

WHAT A WONDERFUL RECIPE!

GLAD YOU LIKED IT, MY BOY... YES, EXCELLENT, BUT IT IS A BIT STRONG... WE WON'T ASK THE GAULS TO DO ANY MORE COOKING EXCEPT ON SPECIAL OCCASIONS. AND NOW LET'S GO TO BED...

I DON'T UNDERSTAND... HOW CAN THEY HAVE LIKED IT?

YOU'RE RIGHT...

IT WAS A BIT INSIPID.

?!

YOU MAY HAVE GOT AWAY UNCRUCIFIED, BUT I'LL HAVE YOU THROWN TO THE LIONS YET... THEY DON'T OFTEN TASTE CHOICE TITBITS FROM THE HOUSE OF TYPHUS, POOR THINGS!

MEANWHILE, SLEEP TIGHT, MY WORKS OF ART! WE RISE AT DAWN IN THIS HOUSE, AND I SHALL KEEP YOUR NOSES TO THE GRINDSTONE!

ASTERIX, DO YOU THINK WE'LL END UP AS CHOICE TITBITS FED TO THE LIONS?

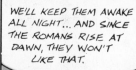

I DON'T KNOW ABOUT THAT, OBELIX, BUT I HAVE AN IDEA THAT WILL MAKE THE ROMANS FED UP WITH US!

WE'LL KEEP THEM AWAKE ALL NIGHT... AND SINCE THE ROMANS RISE AT DAWN, THEY WON'T LIKE THAT.

WE'LL BE SOLD BACK FIRST THING TOMORROW.

IT'S TIME!

HGMFFF— FKHGPFFF!

WE NEED SOMETHING TO MAKE A LOUD NOISE. LET'S TRY THE KITCHEN.

COULDN'T WE MAKE A LOUD NOISE BY SNORING?

BLOING! CLANG! BLOIMM! BLOIM! CLANG!

WHAT'S GOING ON?

THE BARBARIANS! IT'S THE FALL OF THE ROMAN EMPIRE!

CLANG! BLOIMM! CLANG! BLOIMM! CLANG!

BLOIMM! CLANG! BLOIMM! CLANG! CLANG!

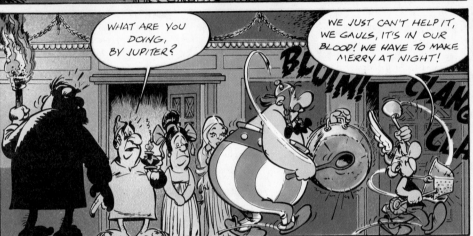

WHAT ARE YOU DOING, BY JUPITER?

WE JUST CAN'T HELP IT, WE GAULS, IT'S IN OUR BLOOD! WE HAVE TO MAKE MERRY AT NIGHT!

BLOIMM!

CLANG

MASTER, WOULD YOU LIKE ME TO HAVE THEM WHIPPED?

WHIP SLAVES FROM THE HOUSE OF TYPHUS? DO YOU THINK GAULS GROW ON TREES?

CLANG! BLOIMM!

WHAT'S ALL THIS? EVERYONE AWAKE?

IS THIS THE SORT OF HOUR YOU CHOOSE TO COME HOME, YOU DISSOLUTE BOY?

JUST IN TIME, TOO! I SEE YOU'RE HAVING SOME FUN IN THIS DOMUS FOR ONCE!

BLOIMM!

CLANG

OH YES! LET'S HAVE THE FUN, LIKE THE GAULS!

I'M GOING TO FIND MY FRIENDS! THEY CAN'T HAVE GOT FAR, NOT IN THE STATE THEY'RE IN!

BUT...

CLANG! BLOIMM!

OH YES, OSSEUS DARLING! LET'S HAVE A SURPRISE ORGY, LIKE WHEN WE WERE YOUNG!

CLANG! CLANG! CL...

?!?

GOLDENDELICIUS! LIGHT THE LAMPS! FETCH SOME WINE! SEND FOR MUSICIANS AND BRING ON THE DANCING-GIRLS!

SOON AFTERWARDS...

CLANG! TZIIING! BLING! HAHA HIHIHI!

I SAY, ASTERIX, DO YOU THINK WE COULD RESELL THESE ROMANS?

25

THE SUN RISES UPON A HOUSE WHICH HAS FINALLY FALLEN SILENT...

COME ON, YOU LOT! BRING OUT YOUR MAPPAE AND SCOPAE!*

* FLOORCLOTHS AND BROOMS

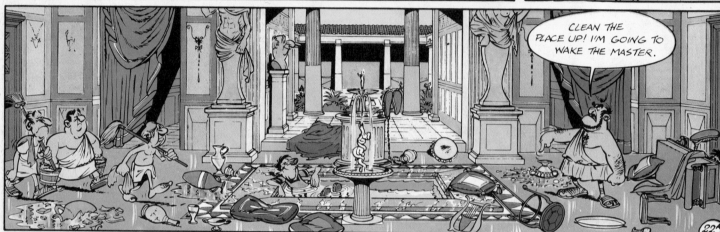

CLEAN THE PLACE UP! I'M GOING TO WAKE THE MASTER.

MASTER, THE SUN IS ALREADY HIGH IN THE SKY. AM I TO SEND FOR THE TONSOR TO SHAVE YOU?

NO! AND TELL ALL THOSE OTHER IDIOTS THAT IF THEY GO ON MAKING THAT NOISE I'LL SELL THEM OFF AS A JOB LOT, WITH YOU AND THE TONSOR THROWN IN!

OOOOH! MY HEAD...

EK...MASTER...MAY I REMIND YOU THAT YOU HAVE AN IMPORTANT ENGAGEMENT AT THE PALACE THIS MORNING? AM I TO GO AND SAY YOU'RE ILL?

HMM? NO...I'LL SEND MY GAULS FROM THE HOUSE OF TYPHUS, THAT WILL LOOK MORE ELEGANT. NOW LEAVE ME ALONE. I FEEL A BIT EX COLORE. CLEAR OFF!

OH, SO THEY'VE SUPPLANTED ME! SO THEY'RE GOING TO THE PALACE INSTEAD, EH? RIGHT! I HAVE AN IDEA!...

THERE'S ONLY ONE WAY OUT OF THIS: WE'LL HAVE TO BUY OURSELVES BACK FROM HUMERUS. THEN WE'LL THINK OF A PLAN TO GET INTO CAESAR'S PALACE. GIVE ME ALL THE MONEY YOU'VE GOT.

THERE YOU ARE...DO YOU THINK THAT WILL BE ENOUGH?

WE ARE FROM THE HOUSE OF TYPHUS AFTER ALL... PERHAPS WE'RE BEYOND OUR MEANS.

WE'LL BEAT HIM DOWN.

HEY, YOU GAULS! THE MASTER WANTS TO SEE YOU IN HIS TABLINIUM.※

HE'S TIMED THAT WELL!

※ STUDY

AH, MY DEAR GAULS... WE REALLY DID HAVE A GOOD TIME WITH YOU LAST NIGHT...

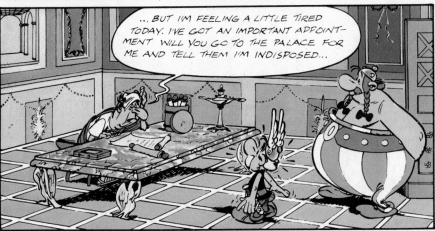

...BUT I'M FEELING A LITTLE TIRED TODAY. I'VE GOT AN IMPORTANT APPOINT-MENT. WILL YOU GO TO THE PALACE FOR ME AND TELL THEM I'M INDISPOSED...

TO JULIUS CAESAR'S PALACE?

YES. ASK FOR LOCUS CLASSICUS, ONE OF CAESAR'S SECRETARIES.

WAIT A MOMENT. WE WERE GOING TO BEAT YOU DOWN...

NO, NO, NO!

AND HURRY BACK, SO WE CAN TRY YOUR FANTASTIC RECIPE AGAIN!

WHAT A STROKE OF LUCK, BY TOUTATIS!

WHAT A STROKE OF LUCK, BY MERCURY!

NOW WHAT? HAVE WE GIVEN UP THE IDEA OF BUYING OURSELVES BACK?

WE DON'T NEED TO! WE'VE GOT A GOOD EXCUSE TO GET INTO CAESAR'S PALACE NOW!

ONCE INSIDE, WE'LL FIND A WAY TO GATHER CAESAR'S LAURELS!

WHAT A PITY! I SHOULD HAVE LIKED TO BUY US... WE WOULD HAVE MADE A NICE SOUVENIR TO TAKE HOME FROM OUR TRIP.

HALT! QUO VADIS?

WE HAVE COME ON BEHALF OF OUR MASTER, OSSEOUS HUMERUS, WITH A MESSAGE FOR...

...FOR LOCUS CLASSICUS, CAESAR'S SECRETARY. COME IN, COME IN! YOU'RE EXPECTED.

TEEHEEHEE-HEE!

?

HE LET US VADERE QUO WE WANTED TO GO VERY READILY... THIS IS EASY!

TOO EASY... HOW DOES HE KNOW WE'RE EXPECTED?

HOLD IT THERE, GAULS!!

?!?...

RIGHT! SHALL WE GET THEM?

NO. LET'S FIND OUT WHAT THEY WANT ANYWAY, THEY COULD HACK US TO PIECES WITH THEIR WEAPONS

HUH! WE'RE OUR OWN MASTERS, AREN'T WE...?

SO YOU WANT TO ASSASSINATE JULIUS CAESAR, DO YOU?

?

AN HONEST SLAVE, WHO WILL BE REWARDED FOR HIS SERVICES, HAS DENOUNCED YOU. HE DISCOVERED YOUR PLOT.

... YOU USED A TRICK TO INFILTRATE THE HOUSE OF OSSEUS HUMERUS, IN ORDER TO FIND A PRETEXT TO GET INTO CAESAR'S PALACE AND KILL HIM!

?

TAKE THEM AWAY TO THE PALACE PRISON!

THE PALACE PRISON...

WE DIDN'T WANT TO KILL OLD JULIUS, DID WE, ASTERIX?

DO YOU DENY YOU HAVE DESIGNS ON OUR HEAD OF STATE?

ONLY WHAT'S ON IT.

WHAT'S THE GOOD OF PROTESTING, OBELIX? WE'RE DONE FOR

TAKE THEM AWAY!

?

29

IN YOU GO!

I DON'T UNDERSTAND, ASTERIX! WHY ARE WE LETTING THEM TREAT US LIKE THIS? THEY'RE ONLY ROMANS, AFTER ALL!

VLAN!

BUT THIS IS WONDERFUL, OBELIX! WE'RE IN THE PALACE! TONIGHT WE CAN GET OUT OF OUR CELL AND LOOK AROUND FOR CAESAR'S LAUREL WREATH AT OUR LEISURE!

WHAT! WE DON'T GET ANY SLEEP TONIGHT EITHER?

CKVII DAYS TILL I GET OUT

NO SEDITIOUS GRAFFITI

GLORIA VICTIS

VERITAS ODIUM PARIT

DEATH TO THE LIONS

AND SO, THAT NIGHT...

OPEN THE DOOR AS QUIETLY AS POSSIBLE.

?

CLONG

CLANG!

THEY MAKE MORE NOISE COMING DOWN THAN GOING UP

LET'S GO!

BIFF!

30

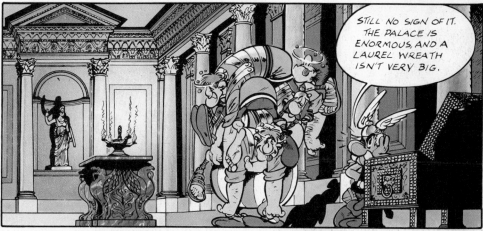

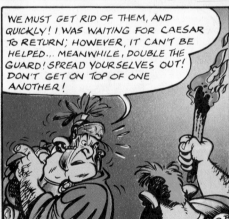

I DON'T LIKE BIG TOWNS; I NEVER SLEEP WELL THERE. I FEEL HEMMED IN... SHUT UP...

WHAT WE MUST DO IS FIND CAESAR... HE'S GENERALLY TO BE FOUND JUST UNDERNEATH HIS LAUREL WREATH.

AH! SO THESE ARE MY CLIENTS!

YOUR CLIENTS?

YES, I'M YOUR LAWYER, TITUS NISIPRIUS.

YOU ARE GOING TO BE TRIED THIS VERY DAY, AND I'VE BEEN ASSIGNED TO YOU AS LEGAL AID. IT'S A GOOD BRIEF FOR ME. TWO GAULISH WIZARDS — THAT'LL ATTRACT A LARGE CROWD!

I HAVE A VERY FINE SPEECH PREPARED. IT BEGINS LIKE THIS: DELENDA CARTHAGO, SAID THE GREAT CATO...

ARE YOU GOING TO GET US SET FREE?

YOU MUST BE JOKING! LOTS OF WILD ANIMALS HAVE ARRIVED IN THE CIRCUS, AND THEY'VE HAD NOTHING SUBSTANTIAL TO GET THEIR TEETH INTO... SO YOU SEE, TWO GAULISH WIZARDS, JUST THINK! WHAT A SHOW!

DOES JULIUS CAESAR GO TO THESE SHOWS?

USUALLY, YES... DELENDA CARTHAGO, I SHALL SAY TO THEM...

AND WHEN HE GOES TO THE CIRCUS, DOES HE WEAR HIS LAUREL WREATH?

I'VE NEVER SEEN HIM IN A STRAW HAT, MY FRIEND... WHY DON'T YOU LISTEN TO MY PLEA FOR THE DEFENCE? DELENDA CARTHAGO SAID THE GREAT CATO...

?

BONG! BONG!

BRING THE GAULISH WIZARDS BEFORE THE COURT!

THE DELATOR ✳ WILL SPEAK FIRST.

✳ COUNSEL FOR THE PROSECUTION

DON'T WORRY.

DELENDA CARTHAGO, AS THE GREAT CATO SAID...

WH...WHAT THE...? DELENDA CARTHAGO? BUT I WAS GOING TO...

SILENCE! YOUR TURN WILL COME; YOU CAN SPEAK AFTERWARDS.

MAY I NOW CONTINUE?

TWO FOREIGNERS WHO HAVE DECEITFULLY INFILTRATED A FAMILY HIGHLY RESPECTED IN THE CITY, WITH THE SOLE AIM OF FINDING A PRETEXT FOR A COWARDLY ATTEMPT ON THE LIFE OF THE ILLUSTRIOUS PERSON OF JULIUS CAESAR...

...AND YOU WASTE YOUR TIME IN FUTILE ARGUMENTS? IN ENDLESS SPEECHES?

I SAY *NOOOO!* JUDGES, I SAY NO! THROW THEM TO THE LIONS! TO THE LIONS, I SAY!

AND MAY CAESAR HIMSELF, WEARING THE LAUREL WREATH HE SO RICHLY DESERVES, WITNESS THE FEASTING OF THESE HARMLESS ANIMALS...

...WHOSE FANGS WILL THUS BECOME THE MIGHTY SWORD OF IMPERIAL JUSTICE...THAT IS THE CASE FOR THE PROSECUTION.

SNIFF! SNIFF! SNIFF! SNIFF! SNIFF! SNIFF! SNIFF! SNIFF! SNIFF! SNIFF!

SNIF!

I—I FIND THE ACCUSED GUILTY. I SENTENCE THEM TO BE THROWN TO THE LIONS IN THE CIRCUS MAXIMUS!

BRAVO! BRAVO! HEAR, HEAR!

BANG!

LONG LIVE THE PRISONERS! BRAVO!

BRAVO! HEAR, HEAR!

NOT EXACTLY A CLASSIC SUMMING-UP BUT SO MOVING!

THOSE WILD ANIMALS ARE LUCKY! VERY, VERY LUCKY!

CLEAR THE COURT! LEGIONARIES, CLEAR THE COURT!

ONE OF THE SINISTER CELLS IN THE CIRCUS MAXIMUS...

TYPHUS HAS SENT YOU THIS AMPHORA OF WINE, AND THESE DELICACIES ARE FROM THE HUMERUS FAMILY...

THAT ROAST BOAR WAS GOOD.

THAT'S THE ADVANTAGE OF BEING THROWN TO THE LIONS. YOU ALWAYS GET TASTY GOURMET DISHES...

WHEREAS THOSE THROWN FROM THE TARPEIAN ROCK GET SOLID, HEAVY FOOD.

THERE'S A FANTASTIC LINE-UP ON THE PROGRAMME: LIONS PANTHERS, LEOPARDS, TIGERS! ALL FINE SPECIMENS! THEY'VE EATEN NOTHING BUT LETTUCE FOR A WHOLE WEEK NOW!

SO YOU HAVE NO CAUSE FOR COMPLAINT! YOU REALLY ARE SPOILT!

CLANG!

ASTERIX, I'M SCARED.

SCARED? SCARED OF A FEW WILD ANIMALS?

OH, I'M NOT WORRIED ABOUT THE ANIMALS, IT'S THE PUBLIC! ALL THOSE PEOPLE!

YOU'LL BE ALL RIGHT IN THE ARENA...

I'M SURE THAT ONCE THE SHOW BEGINS OTHER PRISONERS FORGET THEIR STAGE FRIGHT TOO AND THINK OF NOTHING BUT THE ANIMALS.

I'M AFRAID OF LETTING THE... AUDIENCE DOWN... LOOKING SILLY...

EXCUSE ME, YOU WOULDN'T HAVE A DROP OF OIL TO RUB ME DOWN WITH, WOULD YOU— LIKE THE GLADIATORS? IT LOOKS GOOD.

OIL?

DON'T YOU THINK MUSTARD WOULD BE MORE APPROPRIATE.

THE CIRCUS MAXIMUS IS PACKED WITH THE .USUAL ENTHUSIASTIC FIRST-NIGHT, OR IN THIS CASE LAST-NIGHT, AUDIENCE.

CREEEEAK!

AAAAAAAAHHHH!

IT'S YOUR TURN NOW.

AT LAST!

WHAT'S THAT?

IT'S TO MAKE ME TASTE NICE.

YOU'RE A REAL PROFESSIONAL! ONLY THE GREAT ARTISTES THINK OF SMALL DETAILS LIKE THAT!

ARE MY PLAITS ALL RIGHT?

D'YOU KNOW, PEOPLE COME FROM ALL OVER THE PLACE TO BE EATEN HERE, AND THERE'S NEVER BEEN THIS MUCH EXCITEMENT!

WHAT A PITY JULIUS CAESAR ISN'T HERE FOR THIS PERFORMANCE!

WHAT'S THAT?

CREEEAK!

BIFF! BANG! BIFF!

AREN'T THERE ANY MORE?

THIS ISN'T THE PLACE FOR THAT KIND OF THING! IF YOU WANT TO FIGHT, GO INTO THE ARENA!

WE WANT OUR MONEY BACK! WE WANT OUR MONEY BACK!

LISTEN TO THE CROWD! JUST LISTEN!

FOR PITY'S SAKE, GO INTO THE ARENA! THEY'LL FLATTEN THE CIRCUS! THE CIRCUS IS MY WHOLE LIFE!

OH, VERY WELL, WE'LL GO ON, BUT ONLY TO PLEASE YOU.

THANK YOU! THANK YOU! YOU WON'T REGRET IT!

?

ER... WHERE ARE THE OTHER ANIMALS?

INSIDE THAT ONE!

THIEVES! SWINDLERS! WE'LL WRECK THE CIRCUS!

BURP!

GUARDS! GET EVERYBODY OUT!

EVERYBODY OUT! EVERYBODY, BY JUPITER!

OUT! EVERYBODY OUT!

NOT US! HE DOESN'T MEAN US!

OH, SHUT UP, OBELIX!

THAT MIX-UP GAVE US GOOD COVER. WE'VE SEEN ENOUGH OF THIS PERFORMANCE. LET'S FIND A PEACEFUL SPOT TO SLEEP.

WHAT A GOOD IDEA!

WE SHOULD BE ALL RIGHT HERE. TOMORROW WE'LL THINK ABOUT OUR NEXT MOVE.

AT NIGHT THE ROMAN STREETS, INADEQUATELY PATROLLED BY THE SEBACIARIA (NIGHT WATCHMEN) ARE THE HUNTING GROUND OF SICARII, EFFRACTORES AND RAPTORES, MURDERERS, THIEVES AND MUGGERS OF ALL KINDS.

BY ALL THAT'S UNHOLY! HERE ARE TWO FINE FELLOWS SLEEPING OFF THEIR BOOZE! LET'S LIGHTEN THEIR PURSES!

RRROON!

DO YOU ROMANS NEVER SLEEP?!

BIF!

BANG!

BIF!

ER...YOU WOULDN'T BE THOSE TWO GAULS EVERYONE IS LOOKING FOR, WOULD YOU?

YES, THAT'S US. AND WHO ARE YOU?

HABEASCORPUS, CHIEF OF THE MOST FEARSOME BAND OF CUTTHROATS THE URBS HAS EVER KNOWN.

I HEAR YOU ARE MAGICIANS. YOUR STRENGTH SEEMS TO PROVE IT...WE COULD USE YOU.

WHY NOT? WE DON'T HAVE ANYWHERE TO GO.

PUT ME DOWN, THEN, AND FOLLOW ME.

LET'S GET A MOVE ON. IT'S NEARLY DAYBREAK.

HERE'S OUR HIDE-OUT: THE CATACOMBS. IT'S QUITE SAFE. YOU'LL MAKE OLD BONES DOWN HERE.

TOMORROW NIGHT WE'LL LEAVE A SKELETON STAFF HERE, AND YOU CAN TRY YOUR HAND AT SKULDUGGERY...

WE WORK AT NIGHT AND SLEEP BY DAY.

GOOD DAY, THEN!

SO THAT'S HOW IT'S DONE!

BANG! BIF!

LONG LIVE JULIUSH CAESHAR!

SOON AFTERWARDS...

RIGHT, OFF YOU GO HOME, NOW. WHY DID YOU GET YOURSELF INTO SUCH A STATE, ANYWAY?

TO CELEBRATE THE RETURN OF JELIUS SOOS...ER...JULIUS CAESAR!

JULIUS CAESAR?

HE HAS RETURNED VICTORIOUS FROM HIS CAMPAIGN AGAINST THE PIRATES...TOMORROW THERE'S TO BE A TRIUMPH IN THE STREETS OF ROME!

ARE YOU SURE?

SURE I'M SURE! GOLDENDELICIUS TOLD ME. HE'S GOT HIS EAR TO THE GROUND, HAS OLD GOLDENDE... GOLDENDEWHATISINAME.

AFTER HE DENOUNCED YOU, THEY MADE HIM PERSONAL SLAVE TO JULIUS CAESAR AS A REWARD!

AH! AND WHERE IS GOLDENDELICIUS NOW?

HE STAYED ON IN THAT BAR OVER THERE, BUT WATCH OUT, HE'S AB-SO-LUTE-LY BLOTTO!

LET'S GO!

GOOD IDEA! LET'S GO!

NOT YOU! YOU GO HOME!

AT LEAST GIVE ME THE RECIPE OF THAT FANTASTIC DISH! I THINK I MIGHT BE ILL TOMORROW, AND THEN I WOULDN'T BE ABLE TO GO TO CAESAR'S TRIUMPH...

RIGHT. LISTEN CAREFULLY. AN UNPLUCKED CHICKEN, SOME CARBOLIX SOAP, KIDNEYS...

BAR AURIGARUM

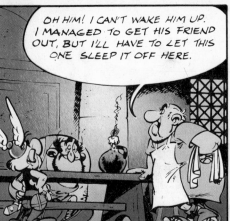

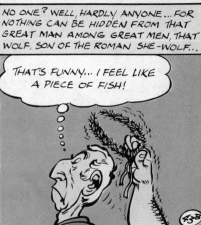

PRINTED IN BELGIUM BY
proost
INTERNATIONAL BOOK PRODUCTION